ISLAND POTTY PARTY

Music and Lyrics by
Tim Friedlander

Illustrated by
W.M. Edwards

ISLAND SHUTTLE

PLAYDATE KIDS PUBLISHING
LOS ANGELES

© 2007 Playdate Kids Publishing
PO Box 2785
Malibu, CA 90265-9998
ISBN-10: 1-933721-15-4
ISBN-13: 978-1-933721-15-6
Printed in Korea
SAN # 6300065
Library of Congress Control Number: 2006935471

Dance in the surf. Play in the sand.
Listen to the rhythm of a steel drum band!

I need to use the potty! I have to pee right now!
Chloe, you're my sister. Will you show me how?

Big kids use the potty when they have to pee or poo.
It's better than a diaper, if you know what to do.

Follow us, little brother, and we'll show you how.
We can have a POTTY PARTY right now!

We're going to a Potty Party, an Island Potty Party.

6

We'll learn at the Potty Party. Have fun at the Potty Party!

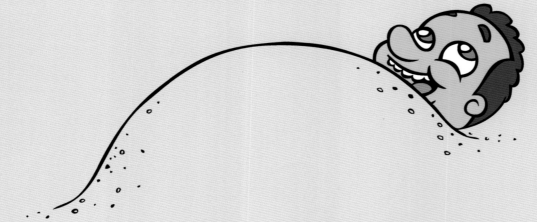

We'll learn at the Potty Party, at the Potty Party today.

Okay, girls. You first!

Well you open the door,

and you put the seat down.

'Cause you don't want

to go on the ground.

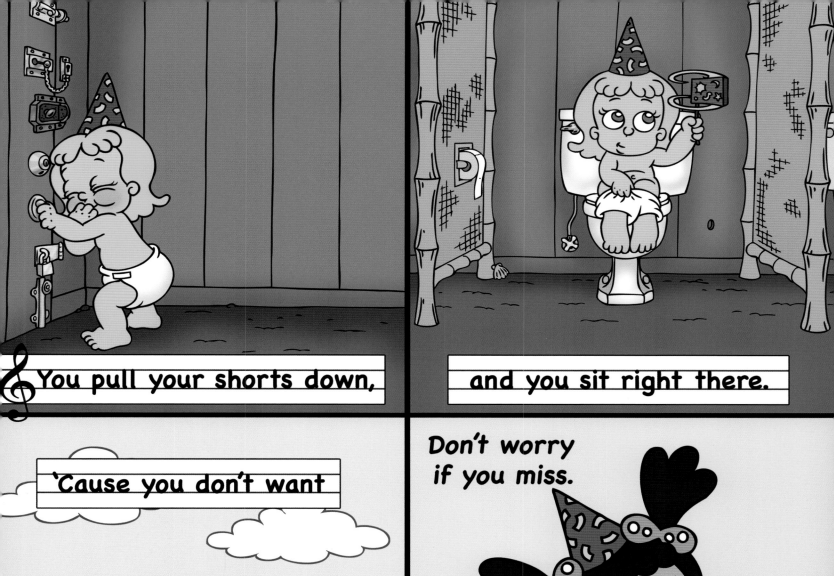

You pull your shorts down,

and you sit right there.

'Cause you don't want

to go in the air.

Don't worry
if you miss.

You can get it
next time!

Okay, boys. It's your turn!

Well you open the door,

and you lift up the seat.

'Cause you don't want

to go on your feet.

You pull down your shorts,

and you aim real straight,

so you don't go

all over the place.

Don't worry if you miss.

You can get it next time!

nd even Mommy and Daddy use the potty.

ven your teacher and your best friend, too!

We went to a Potty Party, a Potty Party today.

 You can have a Potty Party, a Potty Party today.

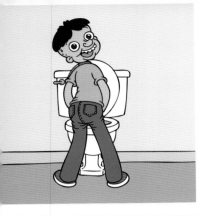

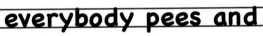
Oh, everybody poops and

everybody pees and

everybody does it every day!

Yes, everybody poops and everybody pees

and everybody does it

EVERY DAY!

EAT, CHEW AND POO!

WHERE YOUR POOP COMES FROM

STEP 1:
You eat food. Food gives you energy to run, jump, play, read— anything!

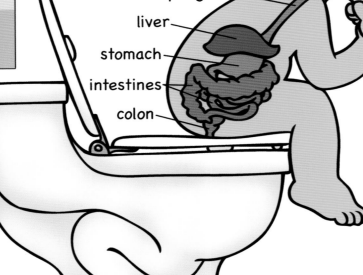

- mouth
- esophagus
- liver
- stomach
- intestines
- colon

STEP 2:
The food travels through your body, and all your different parts take out vitamins and nutrients for you to use as energy.

But always remember: WASH YOUR HANDS!

STEP 3:
You poop or pee whatever is left that your body doesn't need. Then, you flush it away!

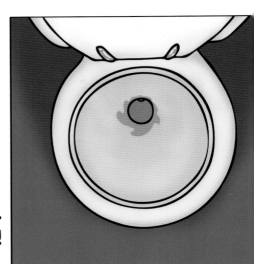

ISLAND POTTY PARTY

Music and Lyrics by Tim Friedlander

We're going to a Potty Party, an Island Potty Party. We're going to a Potty Party, a Potty Party today. We'll

6
learn at the Potty Party. Have fun at the Potty Party. We'll learn at the Potty Party, at the Potty Party today.

Girl Verse: Well you open the door, and you put the seat down.'Cause you

11
Boy Verse: Well you open the door, and you lift up the seat.'Cause you

don't want to go on the ground. You pull your shorts down, and you sit right there.'Cause you don't want to go in the air.

16
don't want to go on your feet. You pull down your shorts, and you aim real straight, so you don't go all over the place.

You can sit. You can stand.

But always remember to wash your hands. You can sit. You can stand. But always wash your hands!

21 2X

Verse 1: Well boys use the potty and girls use the potty and even Mommy and Daddy use the potty. And the babysitters, too, and the doctors do. Even your teacher and your best friend, too!

Verse 2: And the fireman, the policeman, even the lady from the grocery store! And Grandma and Grandpa and the boy over there. Even the funny guy in the chair!

25

Verse 3: And your school bus driver and the mailman, that nice old lady and that big tall man. Well your neighbor, too, and the guy in the hat. And guess what? Even

29

dogs and cats! We went to a Potty Party, an Island Potty Party. We

33
went to a Potty Party, a Potty Party today. We learned at the Potty Party, had fun at the Potty Party.

37
You can have a Potty Party, a Potty Party today. Oh, everybody poops and everybody pees and everybody does it every day! Yes,

41
everybody poops and everybody pees and everybody does it EVERY DAY!

MORE THE PLAYDATE KIDS BOOKS

LET'S BE FRIENDS!

The Playdate Kids
Behavioral themed
coloring and puzzle book
AND animated cartoon DVD set!

The I Like Me Dance
A visit to the zoo
and a self-esteem boost!

Booger Boogie
A jazzy take on
blowing your nose!

Potty Party
A tropical get-together
to learn bathroom skills!

Chloe Nova
Chloe gets a new
baby brother!

Cosmos McCool
Cosmos' parents
get a divorce.

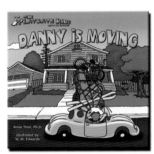

Danny O'Brien
The O'Briens move
to a new house.

Dakota Greenblatt
Dakota's mom goes
to the hospital.

Chloe Nova
Chloe's dog, Marbles,
passes away.

Cosmos McCool
The McCool Family
suddenly grows!

Danny O'Brien
Danny hears a
bad secret.

Dakota Greenblatt
Dakota gets lost
at the mall.